Tales from the
Shop That Never Shuts

Tales from the
Shop That Never Shuts

Martin Waddell

Illustrated by Maureen Bradley

VIKING KESTREL

For Breigeen to read to Tom and
Catherine and James . . . and Joe!

068838

VIKING

Published by the Penguin Group
27 Wrights Lane, London W8 5TZ, England
Viking Penguin Inc., 30 West 23rd Street, New York, New York 10010, USA
Penguin Books Australia Ltd, Ringwood, Victoria, Australia
Penguin Books Canada Ltd, 2801 John Street, Markham, Ontario, Canada L3R 1B4
Penguin Books (NZ) Ltd, 182–190 Wairau Road, Auckland 10, New Zealand

Penguin Books Ltd, Registered Offices: Harmondsworth, Middlesex, England

First published 1988

Printed in Great Britain by
Butler & Tanner Ltd, Frome and London

Filmset in Baskerville (Linotron 202) by
Rowland Phototypesetting (London) Ltd

A CIP catalogue record for this book is available from the British Library

ISBN 0-670-82066-0

Contents

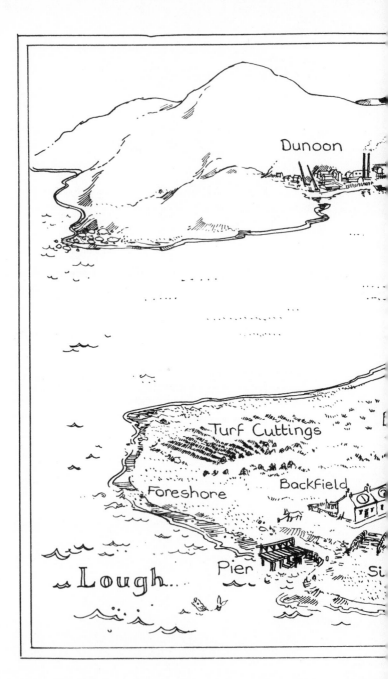

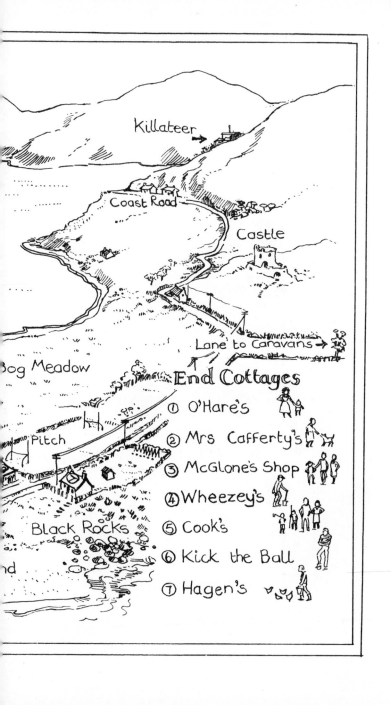

Killateer

Coast Road

Castle

Lane to Caravans →

Bog Meadow

End Cottages

① O'Hare's

② Mrs Cafferty's

③ McGlone's Shop

④ Wheezey's

⑤ Cook's

⑥ Kick the Ball

⑦ Hagen's

Pitch

Black Rocks

This is the McGlone Gang

The Big One is McGlone.
The Wee One is Biddy.
The one giving Biddy a piggy-back is Buster.
Flash is the one with the fish.

1

Pirate Treasure

The Coast Road wound round the foot of the mountain near Killateer, and then ran along the spit of land past Corr's Castle and Maginn's caravan site to the End Cottages, where it stopped. They were called the End Cottages because that is where the road ended, down at the mouth of the Lough.

McGlone lived in the cottage with the Shop That Never Shuts in the front room, which was McGlone's Mammy's Post Office and general store.

McGlone was a very important person, because she was the leader of McGlone's Gang, with Biddy O'Hare in it, and Flash and Buster Cook. McGlone was the leader of the Gang because she was the biggest, and the one who had the most ideas.

Every second Wednesday the library bus came out of Killateer and along the Coast Road to End Cottages, and parked outside the shop.

One Wednesday Buster and Flash and McGlone and Biddy were waiting for it, and they all got on and gave their books to Molly-on-the-Bus.

Then they picked new ones.

Buster got a book on Manchester United, with plenty of pictures.

Flash got *Super Gran.*

Biddy got a picture book about crocodiles, and promised not to chew it, like the last one.

'What book have you got, Mary?' Molly-on-the-Bus asked McGlone. McGlone's first name was 'Mary', but not many called her by it, because McGlone liked being called McGlone, and she bashed people who called her 'Mary'.

'It's a book on Pirates!' McGlone said, and she got it stamped with the library stamp, and went off into the shop to read it, sitting on the tall stool behind the counter.

'Are you not coming out, McGlone?' said Flash, coming in through the shop doorway, and sitting on the paint tins. Biddy and Buster came after him.

'No,' said McGlone.

'Why not?' asked Flash.

'Because I'm minding the shop,' said McGlone.

'You're not minding the shop,' said Buster. 'You're just reading.'

'That *is* minding the shop,' said McGlone. 'Anybody knows that. I'm minding the shop for a minute in case customers come in while my Mammy's out the back.'

'We're in,' Biddy pointed out, settling on the tins beside Flash. There was only room for two on the tins, a big one and a wee one, so Buster missed out.

'You're not customers,' said McGlone, haughtily.

'Yes, we are,' said Flash.

'We are just!' said Biddy.

'Okay!' said McGlone. 'If you are customers what do you want to buy?'

'Sweeties!' said Flash.

'Tons of them!' said Buster.

'All the sweeties in your bottles!' said Biddy, looking at the sweet bottles along the shelf, behind McGlone's head.

'Where's your money?' asked McGlone.

Flash looked at Biddy, and Biddy looked at Buster and Buster said: 'We haven't got any. We're broke.'

'No Credit Given!' said McGlone, and she showed them the sign Mrs McGlone had stuck up on the wall:

NO CREDIT GIVEN
NO CHEQUES
by order
M. McGlone
(Prop.)

'That's just for the caravanners!' Flash said quickly, 'not for us.'

'Everybody down the Cottages gets credit,' said Biddy.

'Baldy,' said Flash. 'And our Mammy.'

'And Mrs Cafferty, said Biddy.

'And Wheezy Roberts,' said Flash.

'And my Mammy,' said Biddy.

11

'And Una O'Hare,' said Buster.

'Una O'Hare *is* my Mammy, Buster,' said Biddy.

'I know she is,' said Buster. 'I was only saying.'

'And Kick-the-Ball!' said Flash. 'They all come in and get things when they need them, and pay for them later, when they can.'

'That's *right*!' said Buster, as though he'd just thought of it.

'Not everybody from the Cottages does,' said McGlone.

'Who doesn't then?' demanded Buster.

'*You* don't!' said McGlone. 'I'm minding the shop while my Mammy's out the back, and what I say goes. Go away!'

They went away, and McGlone kept on reading until her Mammy came in from the back and let her out.

McGlone was all excited, because of what she had read in her Pirate book.

She went round the back and banged her bin, which is what McGlone usually did when she wanted to summon the McGlone Gang, but nobody came.

Then she went down to the pier to see if they were crab fishing, and they weren't, and she went up to the back field to see if they were mushrooming, and they weren't, and she went into the bog meadow to see if they were mudding, and they weren't, and she went to the turf stacks to see if they were hiding, and they weren't, and then she went to the tin hut at the back of Baldy's cottage to see if they were in it, and there was a big notice on the door in Flash's best handwriting.

It said:

So McGlone went in.

'It says "McGlone keep out!" on the door,' Flash told her.

'Well, I'm in,' said McGlone.

'I *told* you it wouldn't work,' said Buster.

'I don't pay any attention to notices!' said McGlone.

'Then you should have let us have credit for our sweets!' said Flash.

'Shut up!' said McGlone.

'Why?' said Flash.

'Because of the Pirates!' said McGlone.

'What Pirates?' said Biddy, anxiously, and she put her sucking thumb into her mouth.

'Bloodthirsty   Cut-You-Up-With-Cutlasses Pirates!' said McGlone, and she made a Cut-You-Up-With-Cutlasses face, which was worse than her own.

There was a long silence, and then Buster said: 'This is another one of your make-ups, McGlone, isn't it?'

'No, it isn't,' said McGlone. 'There were Pirates here.'

'How do you know?' said Buster.

'Are there any *now*?' asked Biddy, looking round in case there was a Pirate hidden in behind McGlone, waiting to pop out and cutlass her.

'There aren't any now,' Biddy, said McGlone, quickly, because she didn't want any Biddy-bother. Biddy was the smallest one in McGlone's

Gang, and she scared easily. 'But there were. I read about them in my book. They were Vikings.'

'Vikings?' said Flash.

'Vikings weren't Pirates, McGlone,' said Buster, slowly.

'What do Pirates do, Buster Cook?' McGlone asked.

'Pirating,' said Buster, who wasn't very sure.

'They go around in boats and they stick swords in people and they steal Treasure!' said Flash. 'That's what Pirates do.'

'So do Vikings,' said McGlone. 'The Vikings came down our Lough from the Irish Sea and they stuck swords in people and took their Treasure, and so they *were* Pirates.'

'*Weren't*,' said Buster.

'Were,' said McGlone. 'It says in my book they were. The very first Pirates.'

'I don't like Pirates,' said Biddy, getting in behind Buster, who was the sort of person it is good to be behind when trouble starts.

'You like Treasure, though, don't you?' said McGlone.

'What Treasure?' said Buster.

'Buried Treasure!' said McGlone.

'I'd like it if we had it!' said Flash.

'But we haven't,' said Buster.

'That's *why* we've got to look for it!' said McGlone.

'Why is why?' said Biddy.

'So we can buy you lots of sweeties, Biddy,' said McGlone.

'You could have given me lots of sweeties if you'd wanted to,' Biddy said, peering round Buster. 'Your shop is full of sweeties.'

'It's my Mammy's shop, and we have to sell our sweeties like anybody else!' said McGlone. 'You'll get plenty of sweeties when we find the Treasure.'

'What Treasure?' asked Buster.

'The Treasure the Vikings hid!' said McGlone.

'If it is hid, how will we find it?' said Buster.

'Get your spades, and I'll show you,' said McGlone.

'You're on!' said Flash, and he flashed away out of the hut.

'This is a daft idea, McGlone!' said Buster.

'If you say I'm daft, I'll spifflicate you, Buster,' said McGlone.

So Buster went off the get his spade, and McGlone went to the Shop That Never Shuts and came back with a spade for herself, and a spoon for Biddy.

'I can't dig with that,' said Biddy. 'It is too small.'

'You can take the wheelbarrow then,' said McGlone.

'What wheelbarrow?' asked Buster.

'Baldy's wheelbarrow for putting the Treasure in!' said McGlone.

'I'll get it!' yelled Flash, and he flashed off again.

17

Flash got the barrow. Buster put Biddy in it and wheeled her off to the Castle after McGlone and Flash.

'What are we going to the Castle for, McGlone?' asked Flash, swinging his spade, because he wanted to get started on the digging.

'To get up on the safe bit of the battlements,' said McGlone, and Buster and Flash and McGlone went up on the battlements. Biddy didn't, because Biddy wasn't allowed on any bit of the battlements; she was too small.

'Start looking!' said McGlone.

'What for?' said Flash.

'Marks on the ground!' said McGlone. 'This is an aerial survey!'

'A what?' said Buster.

'You take an aeroplane, and you fly over where the Treasure might be, and you see dips on the ground where the Treasure hole is, and you mark them on a map, and you go and dig,' said McGlone.

'We haven't got an aeroplane,' Buster pointed out.

'That's why we're up on the battlements, Buster!' said Flash.

'What about the map?' said Buster.

'I'm making the map,' said McGlone, and she showed him her map paper and pencil.

'I'm going down,' said Buster.

'Why?' asked McGlone.

'Because it is too high up, and I might fall off!' said Buster.

'He's a dead loss!' muttered Flash.

'Agreed!' said McGlone.

Flash and McGlone stayed up on the battlements for ages and ages, marking off digging places on McGlone's map. Then they came down and showed it to the other two.

'What's that, McGlone?' asked Buster.

'It's just an old bill from your Mammy's shop,' said Biddy, who was disappointed, because she thought it might have been some Treasure McGlone had found, up on the battlements.

Pirate Treasure!

'It's my Where-To-Dig-For-Treasure Map!' said McGlone.

'It's *our* map!' said Flash, and he showed Buster and Biddy how it worked.

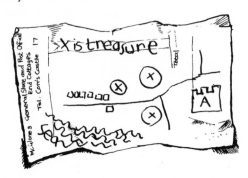

'A is me and McGlone up on the battlements,' said Flash. 'And the Xs are the places where we think the Treasure ought to be.'

'I put the Xs in,' said McGlone.

'I put that one,' said Flash, pointing to the X he had put in.

They went to McGlone's first X, and dug.

'It's all rock!' Flash said, disgustedly.

'The Treasure is under the rock,' said McGlone. 'We'll have to dig it out.'

'Let's try another X first,' said Buster, who had been doing most of the digging. 'It looks a very big rock to me.'

They went to McGlones second X.

'Dig,' said McGlone, and they all started digging.

Then Kick-the-Ball saw them.

Pirate Treasure!

'Hey! Hey, you!' he shouted. 'You're digging up my practice pitch.'

Kick-the-Ball was in the Big Team, and every day he practised out the back, in the field behind his house. It was the best cottage in the row because Kick-the-Ball spent all his time building at it, with things he got off the backs of lorries.

'Your pitch is on top of our Treasure, Kick-the-Ball,' said McGlone.

'And it is going to stay that way!' said

Kick-the-Ball. 'Go and dig somewhere else.'

'We'll just take the Treasure out, and put your pitch back in the hole,' said McGlone reasonably. She didn't want to annoy Kick-the-Ball, because he was the one around the place who moved heavy things when McGlone's Daddy was away on the stone lorry, and they'd all be lost without him.

'What Treasure?' said Kick-the-Ball.

'The Pirate Treasure that we're digging for,' said McGlone.

'That *she*'s digging for,' said Buster, who didn't believe there was any Treasure.

'You were digging too!' said Flash.

'Only because McGlone said she'd bash me!' said Buster.

'That's right,' said Biddy. 'She did.'

'You mustn't go bashing people,' Kick-the-Ball told McGlone. 'And you mustn't go digging fields up either. Go and dig somewhere else.'

'We'll try the X that I put in!' said Flash, who thought that Kick-the-Ball might be getting cross. The day the Rent Man came to argue with Biddy's Mammy, Kick-the-Ball threw the Rent Man's bicycle in the sea, right off the pier. The Rent Man was very cross, but Kick-the-Ball was even crosser, and he chased the Rent Man.

They went off to Flash's X.

They dug and they dug and they dug and they dug at Flash's X, but there was no Treasure.

'All that digging, and what have we got?' moaned Buster.

'A big hole!' said Biddy.

'I'm going home!' said Buster, who was fed up.

'Me too,' said Flash.

'My wee legs are tired,' said Biddy.

'You're No-Use Treasure Hunters!' said

McGlone, but she went home too.

They put Biddy in Baldy's wheelbarrow, and Buster wheeled her back down the road, because of her wee legs.

As they were going down the road, Kick-the-Ball spoke to them over the wall.

'No Treasure?' he said.

'No,' said Flash.

'I knew there wouldn't be,' said Buster.

'And my spoon's bent!' said Biddy, showing it to him.

McGlone was so cross at the No-Use Treasure Hunters that she didn't say a thing for a minute, and then she said: 'There would have been Treasure if we'd dug long enough. It says so in my book.'

'Come over the wall, McGlone!' said Kick-the-Ball.

McGlone went over the wall, and the rest of the Gang came after her.

'Did you look carefully when you were digging up my pitch?' Kick-the-Ball said.

'Yes,' said McGlone and Flash and Biddy.

'No,' said Buster.

'Well, look carefully now,' said Kick-the-Ball.

They looked in the hole on Kick-the-Ball's pitch, and in the grass around it, and in the mud that had come out of the hole, and Biddy shouted: 'MINE!'

She held up a shiny coin.

'Is it Treasure?' asked Kick-the-Ball.

They all looked at it.

It was like this.

Pirate Treasure!

'There's a man on it!' said McGlone.

'A VIKING!' shouted Flash.

'With a ball,' said Buster, doubtfully.

'It is My Treasure, because I found it,' said Biddy.

'Dead right, Biddy!' said Kick-the-Ball.

'I'm going down to the shop to spend it,' said Biddy.

They all went down to the Shop That Never Shuts, and showed Biddy's Treasure to Mrs McGlone.

'It is Pirate Treasure, and Biddy found it!' explained Kick-the-Ball.

'I want a whole lot of sweeties, please, Mrs McGlone,' said Biddy.

'It's only a wee Treasure,' said Mrs McGlone, looking at it.

'I don't know,' said Kick-the-Ball. 'There's enough there to pay for some of *those*, I'd say, and some of *those* and some of *those* and some of *those*, Mrs McGlone.'

'And *those*,' said Flash, pointing at the butter-snaps, because he liked buttersnaps.

'And I dare say some of those as well,' said Kick-the-Ball.

'Well . . .' said Mrs McGlone, doubtfully.

'Any that is not paid for, you can put down to me!' said Kick-the-Ball.

'You're a decent man, Kick-the-Ball!' said Mrs McGlone.

Pirate Treasure!

Pirate Treasure!

She got out her steps, and she climbed up and took down one big jar, and another big jar, and another big jar and another big jar and another big jar and the buttersnaps jar.

She took the sweets out, and put them in a bag.

'Is that all?' asked Biddy.

'There's probably enough for another one,' said Kick-the-Ball, and Mrs McGlone got down the gobstopper jar, and put some in a bag.

'All for me!' said Biddy, looking at the sweetie bags.

'And to share with the other Treasure Hunters!' said Kick-the-Ball.

'If she doesn't, she'll be sick!' said Flash, and McGlone stood on his toe.

They all went out of the shop.

They had five penny chews each, and three gobstoppers each, and six toffee cracknells each, and four mint mallows each, and three cream caramels each, and two buttersnaps each and some jelly babies for their pockets, and that was all.

'Let's go and dig for more!' said Flash.

'NO MORE DIGGING FOR TREASURE!' Kick-the-Ball shouted from the door of the shop. 'The Treasury won't run to it.'

So they didn't go and dig for Treasure.

They went off and skimmed skippystones instead.

Pirate Treasure!

2

McGlone's Monster

One morning McGlone said they were all going to the pier for the McGlone's Gang Crab-Fishing Competition, so they did.

Flash and McGlone had fishing squares and Biddy had her bit of string with bacon on it and Buster had the bucket for the crabs to go in. Buster didn't want to sit on the pier steps, in case he fell in.

Biddy's bacon caught three crabs, a big one and two wee ones.

Flash caught six crabs with his fishing square, but McGlone only caught two.

McGlone got fed up not catching crabs, and then she spotted something.

'It's a Sea Monster!' she shouted.

'What is?' said Buster.

'She is!' said Flash, and McGlone would have bopped him one with her cardigan, only she was too busy jumping up and down and pointing at the sea, beyond the rocks in Hagen's field.

'There it is! There it is!' shouted McGlone.

'Where?' said Flash.

'Out there, off Hagen's field!' said McGlone.

'I'm away to see it!' said Flash, and off he flashed, with McGlone after him, and Buster swinging his bucket.

McGlone's Monster

'I'm left behind!' Biddy shouted, when the other three were already half-way over the sinky sand, heading for the black rocks.

Buster went back for her.

'You're a burden, Biddy!' he said, putting Biddy up on his back.

'I am not,' said Biddy. 'I've just got wee legs.'

Buster carried Biddy down the shingle, and across the sinky sand, where his feet went in up to the ankles, and then he let her down and they scrambled up the black rocks, to join Flash and McGlone.

Flash and McGlone were having a row.

'It was just that old lobster pot, tangled up with the tyre,' said Flash. 'Baldy Hagen uses it for a float.'

McGlone peered at the lobster pot. It was floating just about where she'd seen the Monster, but it didn't look at all like the Monster, close up. Anyway, she'd *said* she'd seen a Monster, and once she'd said it, that was it.

'My Monster was not Baldy's float!' she said.

'Had it great big eyes and yucky teeth and three trillion arms?' said Flash.

'Was it all yellow and covered in goo?' said Biddy, sounding worried. She was sitting down on the black rocks, because her wee legs needed resting, after bouncing all the way on Buster's back.

'N-o,' said McGlone, doubtfully, because she

31

wasn't certain what she'd seen. The Monster, at a distance, had been sort of fuzzy-ish. Things always looked fuzzy-ish to McGlone at a distance.

'What was your Monster like, McGlone?' said Buster.

'Monster-ish!' said McGlone. 'Black as night! With a head like a dragon and teeth like razors and big arms like . . .'

'You're making it up, McGlone!' said Buster, who knew one of McGlone's stories when he heard one. He'd heard a lot of her stories, through being in McGlone's Gang.

'Are you calling me a liar, Buster Cook?' said McGlone.

'Yes,' said Buster.

Then McGlone fell in.

She didn't see the slippery patch on the rock until she stood on it. She was about to *do* Buster, but instead her foot slipped on the rocks, and into the water she went.

WHOOSH!

Splutter! went McGlone, coming back up to the surface.

'I see the Monster now!' said Flash. 'There it is!'

He pointed at McGlone, in the water beside Baldy's float, with the seaweed from the rocks swirling all around her.

'It's H-O-R-R-I-B-L-E!' said Buster.

'Are you drowning, McGlone?' Biddy asked, taking her sucking thumb out of her mouth.

McGlone's Monster

'No,' said McGlone.

'Good,' said Biddy, putting her sucking thumb back in her mouth. 'I wouldn't like it if you got drowned.'

'I'M COMING OUT TO GET YOU!' shouted McGlone, and she scrabbled up the rock and started after Flash and Buster, but they had a head start and were running hard up Hagen's field, away from the rocks.

'I'm left behind!' Biddy wailed, as they all disappeared into the jungle of yellow whins.

Nobody paid any attention.

'Well, if that isn't just like them!' Biddy said, and she took a big breath and hollered, 'I'M LEFT BEHIND!' at the top of her voice, but nobody heard her because McGlone was giving Monster Yells.

McGlone was good at Monster Yells.

'YARROOOOOOGH!'

and

'RRRRRRRRRRRRRRRR!'

and

'YO-OOOOOOOOOOOOOOOOO!' went McGlone, smashing through the whins.

Buster got his pants caught on a bramble outside Baldy Hagen's.

'Pax?' he said, when McGlone caught him.

'You can't say "Pax" to a Bone-Crushing Monster!' said McGlone.

'What do I say then?' said Buster.

McGlone's Monster

'You *scream*,' said McGlone.

Buster screamed.

'I don't call that much of a scream,' said McGlone.

'You scream better then!' said Buster.

McGlone screamed.

'My scream was better than your scream,' she told Buster.

'Wasn't!' Buster said.

'What's all the row about?' said Baldy Hagen, hobbling out of the back door of his house with his egg bucket.

'Buster was screaming,' said McGlone, quickly. 'I was shutting him up.'

'Why was Buster screaming?' said Baldy, putting the bucket down on his back wall, and peering at them in the whins.

'Because McGlone's a Monster!' said Flash, popping up from his hiding place, where McGlone hadn't caught him.

'Oh, well, there now!' said Baldy, and he picked his bucket off the wall, and sloped off to feed the hens.

'I'm a Bone-Crushing Monster, Flash Cook!' said McGlone. 'And I'm after Y-O-U!'

'WAIT! WAIT!' shouted Buster.

'Why?' said McGlone, who felt a bit of bone-crushing was overdue.

'Where's Biddy?' said Buster.

They all looked round.

No Biddy.

'We'll get in real bad trouble!' said Buster.

'BIDDY-HUNT!' shouted McGlone, and they all hared back through the whins and out on to the black rocks, but there was no sign of Biddy.

'Gone!' said McGlone.

'Vamoosed!' said Flash.

'Absolutely vanished!' said Buster.

'Oooooh!' said McGlone, suddenly.

'What is it?' asked Buster.

'The MONSTER!' said McGlone. 'The Monster *ate* Biddy!'

McGlone looked at Flash, and Flash looked at Buster, and Buster said: 'It never did!'

'B-I-D-D-Y!' shouted McGlone. 'B-I-D-D-Y!'

'B-I-D-D-Y!' howled Flash. 'Come here, B-I-D-D-Y!'

The sound echoed round the rocks, and scared the seagulls, but it didn't produce Biddy.

'The Monster never ate Biddy,' said Buster. 'Biddy's just hid.'

'If she just hid, why can't we find her?' said McGlone.

' 'Cause the Monster ate her!' said Flash.

They had another look, round the rocks, and up in the whins, but there was no Biddy.

'It DID!' said McGlone.

'Get Mammy!' said Flash.

The whole Gang fled back to the End Cottages.

'Mammy-mammy-mammy-MAMMY!' shouted

Buster.

'M-A-M-M-Y!' shouted Flash.

'MAAAAAAAA-MEEEEEEEEEE!' shouted McGlone, louder than anybody ever shouted, ever.

'What are you shouting for?' said Buster. 'She's not *your* Mammy.'

''Cause I want her!' said McGlone. ''Cause my Mammy is minding the shop and Biddy's Mammy is away for the Benefit, and your Mammy is the only Mammy left handy, and the Monster ate Biddy!'

'MAAAAAAAAA-MEEEEEEEEE!' they all shouted together, and this time it was louder than the loudest ever, just shouted by McGlone.

Mrs Cook put her head through the window.

'Mammy, McGlone's Monster ate Biddy!' said Flash.

'Did it?' said Mrs Cook.

'Yes!' said McGlone

'Oh well, there now,' said Mrs Cook.

'Are you not going to do something about it?' McGlone demanded.

'About what?' said Mrs Cook.

'The Monster eating Biddy,' said McGlone. 'The Great Big Bone-Crushing Three-Trillion-Arms Monster that came up out of the water and ate our Biddy?'

'She's not *my* Biddy,' said Mrs Cook. 'She belongs to Una O'Hare.'

'Biddy's Mammy isn't in, Mammy,' said Buster.

'That's why McGlone is looking after Biddy.'

'Well, she'd better *look after* Biddy then, hadn't she?' said Mrs Cook. 'Away off and play Monsters somewhere else, for I'm busy.'

She shut the window.

'MAAAAAAAAA-MEEEEEEEEE!' yelled the Gang.

The window opened again.

'This time I'll tell it,' Buster said, quickly.

'What is it?' Mrs Cook said.

'We've *lost* Biddy, Mammy,' said Buster.

'*Lost*?' said Mrs Cook. 'Lost the child?' And the next minute she was down the stairs all at one go, and out the front.

'Where've you lost the child?' she said.

'If we knew where, we wouldn't have lost her, would we?' said McGlone.

'That way! Over the rocks!' said Buster.

'And me thinking it was McGlone's old stories!' said Mrs Cook.

They all ran across Hagen's field and over to the rocks.

'B-I-D-D-Y!' Mrs Cook shouted.

and

'BID-DEEEEE!' shouted the Gang.

Baldy Hagen came through the whins, to see what all the fuss was about.

'They've lost wee Biddy O'Hare!' said Mrs Cook.

'*B-I-D-D-E-E*!' shouted Baldy.

'Oh...oh!' said Mrs Cook. 'Wee Biddy could be drowned, or worse!'

'Eaten!' said Flash.

'By McGlone's Monster!' said Buster, who was beginning to believe in it at last.

McGlone didn't say anything.

She was down off the rocks, looking at the sinky sand.

This is what she saw.

Three sets of footprints coming from the pier, McGlone's and Flash's and Buster's (with Biddy on his back)

and

One set of wee footprints, going back.

McGlone set off after the footprints.

'McGlone!' shouted Flash. 'Where are you going, McGlone?'

'Getting Biddy!' said McGlone.

And she got Biddy.

Biddy was at the pier, with Buster's bucket.

'I put the wee crabs back in the sea, McGlone,' she said.

'Why?' said McGlone.

'Because they didn't like the bucket,' said Biddy.

Mrs Cook and Baldy and Flash and Buster came fussing up.

'BIDDY!' said Mrs Cook, and she scooped Biddy up in her arms. 'Wee Biddy.'

'There now!' said Baldy. 'Not ate at all!'

'I found her,' said McGlone. 'I followed the footprints and I found her.'

'McGlone's a Great Detective!' said Baldy, and McGlone looked very pleased.

'You're all bad, bad children to leave the wee girl behind!' said Mrs Cook, crossly.

'I'm a good child, amn't I?' said Biddy.

Flash and Buster and McGlone and Biddy went back to the Shop That Never Shuts when Mrs Cook had stopped scolding.

'You got us into trouble, Biddy,' said McGlone.

'You're a wee stinker, and I wish the Monster ate you!' said Flash.

'You're all right, Biddy,' said Buster, because Biddy looked upset.

'I just wish I wasn't always the small one,' said Biddy. 'For everybody gets at me!'

'Well, you are!' said Flash.

'I wish there was a *smaller* one for me to look after,' said Biddy. 'Like a wee dog or cat.'

'You're a nuisance, Biddy!' grumbled McGlone.

'I wish I had a puppy like the puppies at Mrs Cafferty's,' said Biddy. 'There's a brown-and-white one I wish I had, for its wee-er than me.'

'Well, you haven't, so there!' said Flash.

'My wee legs are tired,' said Biddy, giving up.

'Tough!' said Flash.

'I want to be lifted!' said Biddy.

'You have my back broke!' grumbled Buster,

so McGlone gave Biddy the piggy-back instead.

'You know *you*, Biddy?' Flash said. 'I don't know why the Great Big Bone-Crushing Three-Trillion-Arms Monster that came out of the water *didn't* eat you!'

'I know,' said Biddy.

'Why?' said all the Gang.

'Because I ATE IT!' said Biddy, who had just as much imagination as McGlone, although she carried it around inside a smaller head.

3

McGlone Gets Glasses

One summer evening McGlone and Biddy and Biddy's Mammy, Una O'Hare, were down by the side of the Lough, getting driftwood on the sled for Biddy's Mammy's fire.

McGlone and Biddy's Mammy got the big bits, and Biddy got the wee bits, to start the fire off with.

'I want a paddle,' said Biddy.

'McGlone will take you paddling when we've got the wood,' said Biddy's Mammy. She knew about not calling McGlone 'Mary', and she never did.

'I want to paddle *now*,' said Biddy.

'Well, away off and paddle then,' said Biddy's Mammy. 'Never you mind if we haven't enough wood to light the fire.'

Biddy went into the tide.

'Och, Biddy!' said McGlone. 'Take your boots off.'

Biddy came out of the tide, and took her wet boots and socks off, and then she went back in again.

'It's a bit late for that now!' said Biddy's Mammy, picking up the soaking socks.

'They'll dry off in front of the fire,' said McGlone.

'If we ever get the fire lit!' said Biddy's Mammy.

'Mammy has firelighters in the shop,' said McGlone.

'There's no way Biddy and me can afford firelighters,' said Biddy's Mammy.

'The wee sticks will do it fine,' said McGlone, and she separated the wee sticks from the big sticks, and then she threw the green ones away, because they wouldn't burn, and pulled off the dry seaweed, which wouldn't burn well either, and would pop in the flames.

A big wave came in.

Biddy sat down in it, *SPLOSH!*

'Biddy!' howled Biddy's Mammy.

'Oh, Mammy!' said Biddy, and the next wave rocked her and wet her hair.

McGlone went right in and rescued her. McGlone wasn't one bit scared of the tide.

'Did you not see the wave coming, Biddy?' McGlone asked her.

'I was looking at the lightship,' Biddy said.

'What lightship?' said McGlone.

'You're all wet through, Biddy, down to your knickers!' said Biddy's Mammy, scooping her up.

'I am,' agreed Biddy.

Biddy's Mammy carried her back to the cottage, and McGlone came behind, dragging the sled, bump-bump-bump, along the shingle, and over the road, and into the cottage.

'You're for bed, Biddy!' said Biddy's Mammy, taking the towel to her.

'I'll away home, Mrs O'Hare,' said McGlone.

'You're a Great Girl helping me, McGlone,' said Biddy's Mammy, and she gave McGlone a doorstep, which is a big piece of soda bread with jam on.

'Is that our blackberry jam?' asked McGlone, munching.

'From the ones we picked?' said Biddy.

It was. Biddy and McGlone and Flash and Buster had picked trillions the last October, and there was still jam in the cottages in July, because Biddy's Mammy made it, and put it away in jars from the Shop That Never Shuts. Mrs McGlone sold some to the caravanners, and the rest they all ate at home. You could smell blackberry all around the End Cottages, when the jam was making.

McGlone went out of O'Hare's, munching the doorstep, but she didn't go home to the Shop That Never Shuts.

Instead she went back to the beach, and stood there squinting out at the tide to see if she could spot Biddy's lightship, but she couldn't.

Buster came up.

'Give us a bite of your doorstep, McGlone!' he said.

'Only a wee bite,' warned McGlone.

Buster took a big bite.

'That's a big bite in your big mouth!' said McGlone, but she didn't bash him.

'Are you feeling all right?' said Buster, wondering why he hadn't got bashed. Everybody bashed everybody in McGlone's Gang, except Biddy. Nobody got hurt; it wasn't that kind of bashing.

'I'm fine,' said McGlone, sounding worried.

'You didn't bash me,' said Buster.

'I can't be bothered to,' said McGlone. 'I'm not interested.'

Buster was surprised, but he didn't say anything.

'Do *you* see any lightship, Buster?' McGlone said.

'Sure,' said Buster.

McGlone Gets Glasses

McGlone Gets Glasses

'Where is it?' asked McGlone.

'Across the mouth of the Lough, where it always is,' said Buster, 'Can you *not* see it?'

''Course I can,' said McGlone, and she went off home, back to the Shop That Never Shuts.

Buster went back to Cook's cottage.

'You know McGlone?' he said to Flash.

'What about McGlone?' said Flash.

'I think she's gone bananas!' said Buster. 'She asked me where the lightship was!'

McGlone went into the Shop That Never Shuts.

It wasn't shut, but it wasn't open. McGlone's shop was in their front room, and it never shut properly, because of the people coming down from the caravans and wanting late lemonade, or gas cylinders, or paraffin, or gobstoppers or stamps. McGlone's shop was a Post Office as well as a shop, with a post box in the wall, and a blue sign outside saying:

YOU MAY
TELEPHONE
FROM HERE

and it had football coupons as well.

'Mammy?' said McGlone, going into the kitchen, through the door from the shop.

'You're all wet!' said Mrs McGlone.

'I was rescuing Biddy from drowning in a Big Tidal Wave!' McGlone said

McGlone Gets Glasses

'Give yourself a medal!' said Mrs McGlone. 'Away in the scullery and dry yourself off.'

'I will in a minute,' McGlone said. 'I just want to ask you something.'

'Fire away!' said Mrs McGlone.

'Mammy, can you *see* the lightship?' asked McGlone.

'Not from where I'm sitting,' said Mrs McGlone. 'I would if I was looking for it.'

'Can *everybody* round here see the lightship?' said McGlone.

'Of course everybody can see the lightship,' said Mrs McGlone. 'Why wouldn't they?'

McGlone thought about it.

Then she said: 'I can't see any lightship, Mammy.'

'Of course you can!' said Mrs McGlone, and she took McGlone out through the kitchen door into the shop, and out of the shop door with the bell on it, and over the road.

They stood on the shore, and Mrs McGlone pointed across the mouth of the Lough, where it opened out to the sea. 'There's the lightship,' said said. 'Just beyond the big buoy.'

'What big boy?' asked McGlone.

'The big red one,' said Mrs McGlone.

'I don't know any big red boy round here. Who is he?' said McGlone.

'Not that sort of boy,' said Mrs McGlone. 'The sort that are out at sea, on the Lough. The buoy marks the channel for the coal boats, down to Dunoon.'

'I can't see it, Mammy,' said McGlone.

Mrs McGlone got worried.

'What can you see?' she said.

'I can see our shore, and I can see the tide, and I can see the black rocks,' said McGlone.

'What about the telegraph pole?' asked Mrs McGlone. 'The one outside Baldy Hagen's?'

'I can see it, sort of,' said McGlone.

'Can you see the wee cross bits on top?' said Mrs McGlone.

'What wee bits?' said McGlone, who could see the pole sure enough, but couldn't make out any cross bits. It was all fuzzy where the wires came together.

'Oh, McGlone!' said Mrs McGlone. 'You need your eyes testing.'

And that's why on Wednesday, which was early-bus day at End Cottages because of the Market in Killateer, Mrs McGlone *shut* the Shop That Never Shuts, and took McGlone off to town.

They went to Mr Reilly the Optician, and he made McGlone sit in his big chair, with her back straight.

'Read that, Mary!' Mr Reilly said. 'Just the top letter.'

McGlone squinted up her eyes, and didn't say a word about not liking being called Mary, because she was too nervous.

There was a big chart on the wall.
It said:

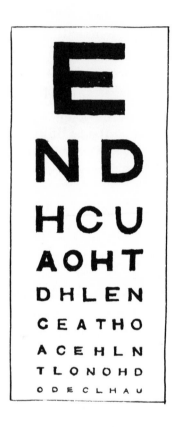

'Read down it if you can, Mary,' said Mrs
McGlone.

'E,' said McGlone, reading the first line.

'Good girl!' said Mr Reilly. 'Try the next line!'

'N D,' said McGlone. 'Then H C U.'

'Down a bit,' said Mr Reilly.

'A D H T,' said McGlone.

'Are you sure of the second letter?' said Mr Reilly.

'D,' said McGlone.

'Ah!' said Mr Reilly. 'Try the next line.'

McGlone couldn't see the next line very well, because the letters were smaller, and looked fuzzy.

'O N L B H,' said McGlone.

'Can you do the next one at all, Mary?' said Mr Reilly.

'It's all fuzzy,' said McGlone. 'I can't make it out!'

'We'll soon set that right!' said Mr Reilly. 'You were right to bring her in, Mrs McGlone. We have a problem here.'

Then Mr Reilly put a big pair of glasses on McGlone, with no glass in the glasses, and he put bits of glass in the holes where the glass ought to go, and each time he asked McGlone to read the chart, and sometimes McGlone could read quite a lot, and sometimes she couldn't. There was another chart with lines on it, like this.

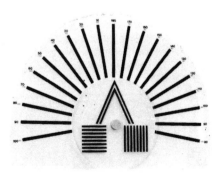

McGlone Gets Glasses

Sometimes, when McGlone looked at it, the lines were all the same, and sometimes they were darker and thicker, depending on what piece of glass Mr Reilly put into McGlone's special glasses.

Mr Reilly did lots of other tests, and there was a light McGlone had to look at, while he looked in her eyes through a special eye-watcher, to see what was wrong with them.

Then he said, 'Well, Mary, we'll have to get you a nice pair of glasses, and that'll put you right as rain!'

McGlone Gets Glasses

McGlone wasn't too pleased, but she picked her frames, and never said a word, because she didn't like any of them, and she didn't like glasses.

Afterwards Mrs McGlone took her for an ice cream in the Ice Cream Shop, and then they caught the bus home.

'I'm getting glasses, Daddy!' McGlone told Mr McGlone, when he came in off his stone lorry.

'Are you?' said her Daddy. 'Isn't that just great?'

'No,' said McGlone.

They had to wait a whole fortnight, and then Mrs McGlone shut the Shop That Never Shuts a second time, and they went off in the bus.

When they came back, McGlone had her glasses on.

'You look great in them, Mary!' said Mrs Cook, 'Wait'll Flash and Buster see you!' McGlone didn't say a word.

'You're like a fancy film star, McGlone!' said Una O'Hare. McGlone didn't say a word.

Kick-the-Ball said the new glasses were great gas. McGlone didn't say a word.

Baldy Hagen said she was like a princess with her glasses on. McGlone didn't say a word.

Mrs Cafferty said it was grand-not-to-see-you-with-your-eyes-all-screwed-up-as-usual-child and it's-a-wonder-nobody-caught-on-sooner-what-ailed-you. Mrs McGlone didn't look too pleased and McGlone didn't say a word.

She went straight into the Shop That Never

Shuts, and sat low down behind the counter on the onion bags, where no one could see her.

'Are you not going out to show your friends your new specs?' McGlone's Daddy said.

McGlone Gets Glasses

'Not now,' McGlone said, wrinkling her nose, and making her glasses spring up.

'Just leave her be,' said Mrs. McGlone. 'It'll take some getting used to.'

McGlone didn't go out for a whole hour, and then she did.

Buster and Flash and Biddy were in Baldy's garden, gathering the eggs.

'Specky four-eyes!' shouted Flash. 'What's life like behind windows, McGlone?'

'You look awful!' said Biddy.

McGlone looked at them. She didn't even feel like bashing anybody. There was a big lump in her throat.

'They're not bad, McGlone,' Buster said, and he looked very hard at Flash, and made a face.

'Eh ... they're not as bad as you think they are, McGlone,' said Flash.

'I think they're awful!' said Biddy.

'Dry up, Biddy,' said Buster.

'I agree with Biddy,' said McGlone.

Then she helped Buster and Flash and Biddy to get the eggs out of the hedge and into Baldy's bucket for him. They put the bucket up on Baldy's

wall when they'd finished, and went off to the shore.

'I can SEE the lightship!' said McGlone, suddenly.

'Where is it, McGlone?' said Buster.

'There!' said McGlone.

It was over at the far side of the Lough, beyond the big red buoy that marked the opening of the channel.

McGlone could see the lightship, and the trees on the other side of the Lough, and lots and lots of houses in Milestown, above the harbour, and the little cross bits on top of Baldy Hagen's telegraph pole, as clear as clear.

'Can you see the colour on that bird's back?' asked Buster.

'YES!' said McGlone.

'So can I,' said Biddy. 'I've been able to see it always, with no specs.'

But McGlone wasn't listening. She was looking about and seeing things, for the first time, without all the fuzzy-ness there used to be about them.

'You know these glasses, Buster?' she said. 'They're just B-R-I-L-L-I-A-N-T.'

'I think they're awful, whatever Buster says!' said Biddy.

'Listen, you, Biddy.' said McGlone. 'Did you know I got two ice creams for getting these glasses? One a fortnight ago, and another big one today for the fitting?'

McGlone Gets Glasses

She told Biddy all about the ice creams, which had bananas and cherries and parasols, and were called Banana Boats, and came in dishes with pink spoons.

'Could I have the parasol?' said Biddy, but McGlone had left it behind.

'Now you can't bash us, McGlone!' said Flash

'Why not?' said McGlone.

'Because we won't be allowed to bash you back, now you've got glasses!' said Flash.

'We'll see about that!' said McGlone, and she took her glasses off and bashed Flash with her cardigan, and then she put the glasses back on.

Biddy went home to her house.

'Mammy?' Biddy said. 'Mammy, could I not have glasses?'

'What for?' said Biddy's Mammy.

'I *want* glasses like McGlone's,' said Biddy.

'McGlone's glasses are very nice,' agreed Biddy's Mammy.

'They're *brilliant*,' said Biddy. 'McGlone can see everything now that she couldn't see before.'

'But you can see without glasses, Biddy,' said Biddy's Mammy. 'What would you want glasses for?'

'You get two ice creams with parasols if you get glasses like McGlone's,' said Biddy. 'That's what I want them for.'

But she didn't get them.

4

The Shop That Never Shuts

One day Wheezy Roberts was trying to hide from the Welfare Man when he fell off the roof of O'Hare's house, *wham-bam!*, on top of Buster.

'You brained me!' said Buster.

'Aaaaah!' moaned Wheezy.

'Wheezy's hurt, aren't you, Wheezy?' said Biddy, who'd been minding the new tiles while Buster held the ladder. Holding the ladder was Buster's job, because Buster was reliable.

'Aaaaaah!' went old Wheezy.

'Are you all right, Wheezy?' said Buster, picking himself up and dusting himself down, for he'd fallen in the turf pile. Biddy's Mammy kept her turf out the back, and Wheezy had the ladder over the turf pile. Wheezy was up on the roof mending the hole in it, when he saw the Welfare Man's car going by, over on the road. Wheezy was supposed to be sick-in-bed sick, so when he saw the Welfare Man's car, he thought the Welfare Man might look out and see him. He tried to get down off the roof in a hurry, but he lost his footing, and fell off the roof right on top of Buster, with a bang.

Flash heard the bang, and he gave up watering Cafferty's goat, and came leaping over the back

McGlone Gets Glasses

wall to see what the excitement was.

'Wheezy's dead!' said Biddy.

'Aaaaah!' went Wheezy.

'No, he's not, Biddy,' said Buster, sensibly, because dead people don't go '*Aaaaah!*' and hold their legs, which is what Wheezy was doing.

'I think his leg is bust!' said Buster. 'Get somebody!'

Flash flashed off to do it. Biddy's Mammy wasn't there, for she was up at the caravan camp cleaning caravans for Mrs Maginn, and Mrs Cook wasn't there, because she was helping on the Meals on Wheels, taking dinners to all the sick people who were supposed to be in their beds like Wheezy, only Wheezy wasn't. Buster ran on down the row, heading for the Shop That Never Shuts, because there was always somebody there.

He met McGlone, who was reading her book on the wall.

'Wheezy Roberts fell off the roof and bust his leg, and I'm to get someone!' Flash announced, feeling important.

The Shop That Never Shuts

'We'll get my Mammy!' said McGlone, and she belted into the shop and got Mrs McGlone out from behind the counter, where she was counting the second-class stamps.

'Oh, Mother-of-God!' said Mrs McGlone, and she threw down the stamp book on the counter and dashed out of the door.

'Mind the shop!' she yelled at McGlone.

'I'm minding it,' said McGlone.

Flash and Mrs McGlone went running up the row to Biddy's house, and then Flash came flashing back again to the Shop That Never Shuts.

'Your Mammy, Mrs McGlone, says ring the ambulance, McGlone!' he panted, and then he said: 'How do you ring the ambulance, for I've never rung it?'

'Watch me!' said McGlone, because she knew all about telephones, working in the Shop That Never Shuts, which had the YOU MAY TELEPHONE FROM HERE sign outside, and a telephone inside.

Nine-nine-nine, McGlone dialled.

'Emergency Services. Which service do you require?' asked the voice on the phone.

'Ambulance!' said McGlone.

'What number are you speaking from?' said the voice, and there were a whole lot of clicks.

'Corr's Castle 17,' said McGlone, because that was the number on the telephone, although McGlone didn't know where the other sixteen phones were, for they weren't at End Cottages.

'You're doing great, McGlone!' whispered Flash, who was very impressed.

'It's easy!' said McGlone. 'I saw my Mammy do it before, when the caravanner fell off his bicycle!'

'Ambulance!' snapped a new voice on the phone.

'Hullo,' said McGlone. 'This is Mc... Mary McGlone speaking. From the End Cottages. Mrs McGlone's Post Office. Wheezy Roberts fell off the roof of Una O'Hare's house and bust his leg and my Mammy, Mrs McGlone, says would you send an ambulance quickly?'

''Cause he might die,' whispered Flash.

''Cause he might die,' added McGlone.

'What number are you calling from?' asked the voice.

'I already told the other one that,' said McGlone, impatiently.

'Number, *please*,' said the voice.

'Corr's Castle 17,' said McGlone.

'It'll be with you directly,' said the voice, and McGlone put the telephone down.

'That was B-R-I-L-L-I-A-N-T, McGlone!' said Flash.

'Anybody can work the phone,' said McGlone.

'Anyone that's got one can,' said Flash.

'Away and tell my Mammy it's all right, for I've got to mind the shop,' said McGlone, and Flash flashed off.

Biddy came in, and set the door bell jingling.

'Wheezy broke his leg,' she told McGlone. 'But he won't die. Buster says so.'

'Good,' said McGlone.

The telephone rang again.

McGlone picked it up. 'Corr's Castle 17. Can I help you?' she said.

'This is the Exchange,' said a new voice. 'Did someone there call for an ambulance?'

'Yes,' said McGlone. 'I did it. And the

ambulance had better come quick, for Wheezy has his leg broke.'

'Is that Mary McGlone?' said the voice.

'It is,' said McGlone, not mentioning anything about the 'Mary'.

'Where's your Mammy?' demanded the voice.

'Up looking after Wheezy Roberts,' said McGlone. 'She told me to ring.'

'Oh,' said the voice. 'Just checking it wasn't a joke call.'

'I don't make joke calls,' said McGlone. 'I make calls seriously. This is a Post Office, you know!'

'Don't I just!' said the voice.

'Well, I hope your ambulance will be here soon,' said McGlone.

'How's the new glasses?' the voice asked.

'They're doing fine,' McGlone said.

'Grand!' said the voice. 'Give my regards to your Mammy!'

The phone clicked dead.

'That was an ignorant phone call, that was,' said McGlone.

'Why?' said Biddy, who was sitting there on the paint tins, most impressed with McGlone using the phone.

'I don't know who it was,' said McGlone. 'How can I give its regards to my Mammy, when I don't know who was speaking? And there was no call to be personal about my glasses. That's no way to use a phone!'

The Shop That Never Shuts

'You're dead good on phones, McGlone,' said Biddy, admiringly.

'That's because our house is a Post Office,' said McGlone, picking up the stamp book, and sitting down on her mother's stool to count stamps. 'Not everybody is as good at phones as me.'

Biddy went out and sat on the gas cyclinders outside the Shop That Never Shuts, and waited for the ambulance to go by. McGlone locked the stamp book up in her mother's drawer, and then she came out and joined Biddy.

'Why was Wheezy hiding from the Welfare Man, McGlone?' asked Biddy.

'Because he's sick,' said McGlone. 'Supposed to be sick-in-bed sick with his chest, only he was out fixing the roof to help your Mammy.'

'My Mammy's not good at roofs,' said Biddy. 'She can do holes in the wall, though. She's a great hand at plaster.'

'Now Wheezy is fell-off-your-roof sick,' said McGlone. 'He'll have to tell the Welfare Man he fell out of bed.'

'Had he his bed on our roof?' asked Biddy.

'No,' said McGlone.

'I don't understand,' said Biddy.

'I didn't think you would,' said McGlone.

There was a ding-ding-ding and the white ambulance came tearing down the Coast Road, sweeping past the Shop That Never Shuts and right along the row to the end, where Buster stopped it.

The man got out and talked to Buster, and then Buster went and moved Cafferty's goat, so that the ambulance could back in behind the cottages, where Biddy and McGlone couldn't see it.

'Buster did great!' said Biddy.

'You can count on Buster,' said McGlone.

'I'm going up to see,' said Biddy.

'No, you're not!' said McGlone. 'You stay with me, and you won't get in trouble.'

Ten minutes later the ambulance pulled out from beyond O'Hare's cottage, and came down the row, where it stopped in front of the Shop That Never Shuts.

The back door of the ambulance opened, and Mrs McGlone stuck her head out.

'You stay where you are and mind the shop!' she called to McGlone. 'I'll be back in a wee while.'

Then the ambulance started off, and ding-ding-dinged its way up the road, shaking the yellow whins, and scaring all the seagulls in Baldy Hagen's field.

'Is your Mammy sick too?' Biddy asked McGlone. 'Did she fall out of bed like Wheezy?'

'No,' said McGlone.

Buster and Flash came up.

'I'm minding the shop!' McGlone announced. 'So I won't be playing.'

'You're too wee to mind the shop,' said Flash.

'Much too wee,' said Buster.

'She isn't, because her Mammy said,' said Biddy.

The Shop That Never Shuts

'I minded the shop many a time,' said McGlone, and she got up from the gas cylinders and went inside and sat on her Mammy's high stool behind the counter, just to show she was properly minding the shop.

'What'll we do?' said Buster.

'We'll mind the shop too!' said Flash.

Flash and Biddy went in and sat on the paint tins, where there was room for a big one and a wee one, and Buster sat on the potato sack.

'We're helping you to mind the shop, McGlone,' Flash said, because it was his idea.

'Don't sit on my potatoes, then!' said McGlone, looking at Buster.

The Shop That Never Shuts

'What else is there to sit on?' said Buster.

'Your backside!' said McGlone.

'That's very rude,' said Biddy.

'They're my potatoes that I'm looking after,' said McGlone, settling her glasses firmly on her nose. 'They're not for sitting on. And neither is my paint!'

Flash and Biddy stood up quickly. Buster thought about it, and then he got up off the potato sack.

'I'll get you later, Buster, for sitting on my potatoes,' said McGlone, grandly. 'I can't get you now because I'm too busy shop-minding.'

Then Biddy's Mammy came in, on her way back from caravan cleaning.

'McGlone said a bad word, Mammy,' said Biddy.

'Did she?' said Biddy's Mammy.

'I didn't!' said McGlone.

'McGlone said "backside", Mammy,' said Biddy.

'That's right!' said Flash.

'She did!' said Buster.

'Buster was sitting on my potatoes,' said McGlone.

'You were quite right, McGlone,' said Biddy's Mammy. 'Do you need me to give a hand with the shop, while your Mammy's off in the ambulance?'

'I do not,' said McGlone, grandly, and then she added, 'Maybe I can get you something, Mrs

O'Hare?' very politely, for she knew how to mind shops, even if she had never minded the shop for more than a small bit at a time.

'Potatoes,' said Biddy's Mammy.

'Half a stone of potatoes, please.'

'Sat-on ones, or not-sat-on ones?' asked McGlone.

'Not-sat-on ones,' said Biddy's Mammy, and McGlone weighed them on the shop scales and put them in a bag for her.

'Put it in the book,' said Biddy's Mammy, and McGlone got her Mammy's Red Book out from under the counter and wrote:

--½ stone potatoes Una O'Hare---

in her best writing, across the page.

'If we bought sweeties, could we put them in the book?' asked Flash.

'I told you before. No Credit and No Cheques,' said McGlone.

'We haven't got any cheques,' said Flash.

'We won't get cheques till we're grown up and millionaires,' said Buster.

'You're not getting any credit either!' said McGlone. Then a caravanner came in for some gas.

McGlone charged him, and she got the money, and gave him his change, and Buster helped him put the gas cylinder in the back of his car.

'A great helper you have there!' said the caravanner, and he gave Buster 10p.

The Shop That Never Shuts

'What about me?' said Flash, but the caravanner didn't hear him.

Baldy Hagen came and bought some nails and string and turpentine, and McGlone wrote it all down in her Mammy's Red Book.

'You're a born shop-keeper!' Baldy said.

Then Kick-the-Ball came in and collected his football pools coupon, and bought some chewing gum. He gave a bit of the gum to Buster, and a bit to Flash, and a bit to Biddy, and a bit to McGlone.

'That's 2p off the price!' he told McGlone, but she didn't let him have it.

Buster and Flash and Biddy went and sat outside on the gas cylinders, and blew bubbles with their chewing gum. McGlone didn't come outside,

because she had to mind the shop. She stayed inside and blew *bigger* bubbles.

The Post Office van came, with the letters.

'Who is in charge of this Post Office?' asked the Postman.

'I am,' said McGlone, putting her glasses straight. 'I'm minding things for my Mammy!'

'There's your deliveries then!' said the Postman, and he handed McGlone the letters for all the End Cottages, and then he drove away.

Buster and Flash and Biddy came in, and walked up to the counter.

'Shop!' shouted Flash.

'Shut up or I'll bash you!' said McGlone, who had her glasses firmly in place, like a real Postmistress, and was reading the addresses on the letters.

'That's no way to talk to customers!' said Flash.

'You're not customers!' said McGlone, impatiently.

'Yes, we are!' said Biddy.

'We've got 10p!' said Flash,

'*My* 10p!' said Buster.

'*His* 10p, and *we're* spending it!' said Flash.

'Only 'cause I let them,' said Buster,

'You're very good, Buster,' said Biddy.

They bought three chews, and three Big Drops.

'One each,' said Buster, and he gave a chew and a drop to Flash, and a chew and a drop to Biddy, and kept a chew and a drop for himself.

The Shop That Never Shuts

'What about me?' said McGlone.

'You don't get any, McGlone!' said Flash. 'You're the shop-keeper!'

'But you can have a bit of mine,' said Biddy, when she saw how disappointed McGlone looked.

'It's all chewed already,' said McGlone.

'Not this bit,' said Biddy, and she pulled off the unchewed half of the penny chew, and gave it to McGlone.

'Thank you very much, Biddy,' said McGlone.

They all chewed.

'What are you doing, McGlone?' asked Buster.

'Looking at the letters,' said McGlone.

'We could deliver them!' said Flash, getting excited.

'People come in and get them,' said McGlone.

'If this was a proper Post Office, the letters would get delivered!' insisted Flash.

'He's right, McGlone,' said Buster.

McGlone thought a bit, and then she said: 'Okay! Let's deliver them!'

So Buster was Postman for Kick-the-Ball and Baldy, and Flash was Postman for his Mammy and Mrs Cafferty, and Biddy was Postlady for her Mammy.

'What about me?' said McGlone.

'You don't get any letters!' said Flash, scornfully.

'Because you are the Postmistress, and you run it!' said Buster.

They delivered all the letters, and Mrs Cafferty

gave Flash 2p and said he could deliver her letters every day if Mrs McGlone let him. Buster didn't get anything, because there were no letters for Baldy, and Kick-the-Ball gave his letter back, because it was a bill and he didn't want it.

'What'll I do with it?' Buster asked.

'Don't know and don't care!' said Kick-the-Ball, so Buster took it back to the Post Office and posted it in the box outside, because it didn't belong to him, and Kick-the-Ball didn't want it, so it must belong to the Post Office.

'Did you put a stamp on?' McGlone asked.

'It had a stamp on already,' Buster said, so that was all right.

Flash bought two more penny chews with his 2p, and kept them all for himself, because the 2p was his postman wages.

Buster didn't get any wages, so he couldn't buy anything.

'What did you get for giving your Mammy the letter?' Buster asked Biddy.

'A Big Kiss!' said Biddy.

'You can't buy anything with that!' said Flash, scornfully.

'It was very nice, anyway!' said Biddy.

Then some caravanners came on their bikes and bought lemonade. Buster and Flash minded the bikes while the caravanners were drinking the lemonade, but the caravanners didn't give them anything.

The Shop That Never Shuts

The Shop That Never Shuts

Biddy went home for her tea.

A man came in a car and asked the right road to the caravan camp, and Flash showed him where the lane down to the camp was, but he didn't give Flash any money.

Flash went home.

'There's only us now, minding your Post Office,' Buster told McGlone.

Then a woman came and tried to sell McGlone eggs from a van, but McGlone wasn't buying any, because they got all their eggs from Baldy Hagen's hens, but the woman didn't know that because she was from Killateer.

Buster went home for his tea.

'Now there's only me at last, minding the Post Office,' said McGlone.

She sat there and didn't eat a single penny chew, until her Mammy came.

Mrs McGlone came through the door of the Shop That Never Shuts, and the bell rang.

'Shop?' she said.

'Can I get you something?' said McGlone, waking up.

'You can get me my soft slippers!' said her Mammy, and they both went through the door into the kitchen. They had tea and soda bread and special scones, while Mrs McGlone told McGlone all about taking Wheezy to hospital and how his leg was, and McGlone told her Mammy all about how the Shop That Never Shuts never shut, for she was busy Postmistressing and shop-keeping all day long.

Then McGlone's Daddy came in for his tea off the stone lorry, and he heard about it too.

'That's brilliant, Mary!' said McGlone's Daddy.

McGlone helped her Mammy bank the fire. Then she went into the shop and took the stamp book out of the drawer and locked it in the safe, and then she went to bed.

'You know what?' she told the bed post, climbing in. 'You know me, McGlone? I was a proper Postmistress and shop-keeper the whole day long!'

And then McGlone went to sleep, and dreamt about it!

5

Biddy's Birthday

'You know Biddy?' said McGlone. 'It's her Birthday tomorrow.'

'Good,' said Buster.

'That'll mean a Party!' said Flash.

'No, it won't,' said McGlone.

'Why not?' said Flash.

'Because Biddy's Mammy has no money, so there won't be any Birthday Party,' said McGlone.

'Poor wee Biddy!' said Buster.

'Poor us!' said Flash, who liked Birthday Parties but didn't get to many, because there were only Buster and Flash and McGlone and Biddy at the End Cottages. McGlone always had a Party, and that was good, and Flash and Buster shared one, half-way between their real Birthdays, but that only made two, and Biddy's Birthday should have made three Parties, but Biddy wasn't having one.

'You know us?' said McGlone.

'What about us?' said Buster.

'We could give Biddy a Birthday Party ourselves!' said McGlone.

They sat on the pier and though about it.

'We haven't any money either,' said Buster.

'You don't need money to give Birthday Parties,' said McGlone.

'Biddy's Mammy thinks you do!' said Buster, sensibly.

'Mammies like to give *proper* Parties,' said McGlone. 'We're not Mammies, so we can give her our sort of Party!'

'Right!' said Buster.

'You're on!' whooped Flash.

'And I'll bash anybody who tells Biddy!' said McGlone, but she kept her glasses on, so Buster and Flash didn't take the threat seriously.

'Where'll we give it?' said Flash, bouncing about.

'Our wee house,' said McGlone.

'We haven't got a wee house,' said Buster. 'Just the cottages.'

'We can't give a party in the cottages, because of the Mammies,' said McGlone. 'That's why we're giving it in our wee house.'

'*What* wee house?' objected Buster. 'You *know* we haven't got one!'

'We'll build one!' said McGlone.

'G-R-E-A-T!' yelled Flash.

Biddy's Birthday

That's why, when Biddy went looking for McGlone and Buster and Flash up and down the row, she couldn't find them. They weren't in the tide, swimming, and they weren't on the pier, fishing, and they weren't in the boats, mucking about, and they weren't in the back field, and they weren't up at the Castle. At least Biddy *thought* they weren't up at the Castle, but she couldn't be sure, because she wasn't allowed to go up to the Castle without McGlone to look after her, so she couldn't be certain, except that they weren't at the bit of the Castle she could see, standing on Kick-the-Ball's wall.

'They're not about, Mammy,' she told her Mammy. 'They've left me behind.'

'McGlone wouldn't do that, Biddy,' said Biddy's Mammy. 'You know McGlone is very good. She always looks after you when I'm busy.'

'So does Buster,' said Biddy.

'Buster's good too, and Flash,' said Biddy's Mammy. 'They all look after you.'

'They're fed up with my wee legs,' said Biddy. 'They're *always* saying it.'

'What's wrong with your wee legs?' said her Mammy.

'Sometimes I won't walk on them,' said Biddy.

'Why not?' asked her Mammy.

'Because my legs *are* wee, and they get tired before anybody else's,' said Biddy.

'Well, you'd better go and practise walking on

them, Biddy,' said her Mammy. 'Away off, because I've Something Special to do.'

Biddy went out of the house, and had a practice walk all along the row, and a practice walk back, and there and back again, so she'd been four times the length of the row, but it didn't do her any good, because there was no sign of McGlone and Buster and Flash.

'No friends!' she told her Mammy.

'Just go and take another look for them, Biddy,' said her Mammy, carefully keeping Biddy away from the kitchen door, so that she couldn't see what was on the table. 'Take your wee legs for a walk. Then you can get wee-leg practice, and find McGlone.'

So Biddy took her legs for a walk along the tide, as far as Kick-the-Ball's broken boat, but she didn't find McGlone. She couldn't go for a paddle, because she wasn't allowed to go for a paddle without McGlone, and she couldn't go and look in Baldy's hut in case they were hunting for eggs because she was scared of hens, and she couldn't go to the Castle because the Castle was out-of-bounds-too-dangerous-for-Biddy-on-her-own, and so she got fed up.

She went to see *Mrs* McGlone instead.

She went in and sat on the potato sack.

'Don't say any rude words!' she told Mrs McGlone.

'Like what?' said Mrs McGlone.

'Like I'm not allowed to say it,' said Biddy.

'I see,' said Mrs McGlone.

'McGlone did,' said Biddy. 'McGlone said it to Buster when he was sitting on the potatoes and McGlone was being Postmistress.'

'She never did!' said Mrs McGlone.

'She did, but I'm not,' said Biddy. 'I don't say rude words.'

'Good,' said Mrs McGlone.

'Where's McGlone?' asked Biddy.

'I don't know,' said Mrs McGlone.

'I'm fed up with these legs,' said Biddy, looking at them.

'They look nice legs to me,' said Mrs McGlone.

'They're *wee*,' said Biddy.

'They'll get bigger,' said Mrs McGlone.

'When?' said Biddy.

'A bit bigger every day, Biddy!' said Mrs McGlone.

'A *bigger* bit bigger tomorrow?' asked Biddy, hopefully.

'Why tomorrow?' asked Mrs. McGlone.

'Because tomorrow is my Birthday!' said Biddy, and she went off to tell Kick-the-Ball about it, in case he knew where McGlone was.

'I haven't a baldy, Biddy!' said Kick-the-Ball.

'What's a baldy?' said Biddy. 'Is it like Baldy Hagen, with no hair?'

'No,' said Kick-the-Ball. '*I haven't a baldy* is a way of saying *I don't know*.'

Biddy's Birthday

'You're not much use, are you?' said Biddy, and she went off.

Mrs Cafferty was taking Wheezy his soup when Biddy found her.

'Why are you taking Wheezy his soup?' Biddy asked.

'Because his leg is broke,' said Mrs Cafferty.

'Does he make soup with his leg?' asked Biddy.

'He puts soup in him to fill up his leg, Biddy,' said Mrs Cafferty. 'That makes his leg better.'

'Is that why your legs are all old, Mrs Cafferty?' said Biddy. 'Or is that just your tights?'

'It's just my tights, Biddy,' said Mrs Cafferty, and she hitched her tights up, so they didn't sag around her ankles the way they usually did.

'Now you'll get yourself a man,' said Biddy.

Biddy's Birthday

'I don't want a man, Biddy,' said Mrs Cafferty. 'I had one, and I don't want another one! Women are best!'

'Like McGlone?' said Biddy.

'Exactly like McGlone,' said Mrs Cafferty, but she didn't know where McGlone was, when Biddy asked her.

Biddy went back to her house.

'What happened to Mrs Cafferty's man, Mammy?' she said.

'Mr Cafferty died, Biddy,' Biddy's Mammy said.

'Well, she doesn't want another one,' said Biddy.

'She must be very choosy,' said Biddy's Mammy.

'I want some soup,' said Biddy.

'What for?' said her Mammy, carefully closing the kitchen door again.

'To fill up my wee legs for my Birthday and make them big!' said Biddy.

'That'll do for our tea then, for we haven't anything else!' said her Mammy.

'Why haven't we anything else?' said Biddy.

'Because I've spent all the Benefit money,' said her Mammy. 'All there was of it, which wasn't much.'

'What about the cleaning-caravans money?' Biddy asked.

'Shush now,' said Biddy's Mammy. 'There isn't supposed to be any cleaning-caravans money. Don't let the Welfare Man hear you.'

'He isn't here,' said Biddy.

'It's just as well!' said her Mammy.

'Am I getting soup?' said Biddy.

And she got it, but she didn't get it in the kitchen. Her Mammy brought it out to her, and never let her through the kitchen door, for she didn't want Biddy seeing what was in there.

The next morning McGlone came round for Biddy early, after she'd finished doing Baldy's hens.

'Happy Birthday, Biddy!' she said, and she gave Biddy a parcel.

It was a very small parcel.

There was a yellow gobstopper in it.

'T-h-a-n-k-o-v-e-r-m-u-c-h!' said Biddy, with the yellow gobstopper in her mouth which stopped her saying 'Thank you very much', which was what she wanted to say.

They went down on the shore, and Buster came up.

'Happy Birthday, Biddy,' he said, and he gave Biddy a parcel.

It was a very small parcel, done up in red paper, with a ribbon on it. It took Buster ages tying the ribbon.

There was a red gobstopper in it.

'T-h-a-n-k-o-v-e-r-m-u-c-h,' said Biddy, putting the second gobstopper in on top of the first one.

Then Flash came up, and gave Biddy a paper-bag with 'FOR BIDDY FROM FLASH' on it.

Biddy's Birthday

'Is there *another* gobstopper in it?' Biddy said.

'Yes,' said Flash.

'Thank you very much,' said Biddy, properly this time, because she'd finished the first two gobstoppers. She put the third in her pocket for later. It was pink.

'*Happy Birthday to you!*
You belong in a Zoo,
With the monkeys, and the donkeys,
And the big kangerooooo!'

sang all the Gang.

'Is that all?' said Biddy.

'All what?' said McGlone.

'All I'm getting for my Birthday?' said Biddy.

'NO!' said McGlone.

'What else am I getting then?' said Biddy. 'Where is it?' And she looked all around, but she couldn't see any more presents.

'Close your eyes and come with us, and you'll see!' said McGlone.

Biddy closed her eyes, and McGlone and Buster and Flash took her round the back of Kick-the-Ball's house and up to the Castle, and then McGlone said: 'You can open your eyes now, Biddy!'

Biddy opened her eyes.

'What is it?' she said, looking at the pile of old driftwood and fish boxes and tyres from the sea that was set against the far side of the Castle wall.

'It's your Birthday House!' said McGlone.

Biddy's Birthday

'Is it?' said Biddy.

'Me and McGlone made it!' said Flash.

'And me,' said Buster.

'Look inside,' said McGlone.

Biddy went inside.

'It's brilliant!' she said.

Then they all got inside the Birthday House, and McGlone showed Biddy where the cupboard was, and the bed, and the chairs and the table.

This is the cupboard.

This the bed.

These are the chairs.

And this is the table.

Biddy's Birthday

This is what the Birthday House looked like inside.

Biddy's Birthday

And this is what it looked like outside,
with McGlone's bottom stuck in the kitchen door,
and Biddy's head looking out of the front door.

Biddy's Birthday

'It's a great house!' said Biddy.

'We built it!' boasted Flash.

'McGlone got the tyres,' said Buster. 'And Flash got the boards, and I got the fishboxes.'

'And I got the cups and saucers,' said McGlone.

She had the cups and saucers on the table, and she took the bottle of lemonade from the cupboard with the biscuits. They all came from the Shop That Never Shuts, after McGlone told her Mammy about making the Birthday House for Biddy.

Then Biddy ate her biscuits and she got up ... just about, because there wasn't much room in the Birthday House ...and she looked at her legs.

'Are they any bigger?' she asked McGlone.

'Not much,' said McGlone.

'I thought they would be bigger,' said Biddy.

'I'm sure you will get bigger, Biddy,' said Buster.

'I thought I'd get bigger on my Birthday,' said Biddy. 'For there's nothing else.'

'What do you mean nothing else?' said McGlone

'My Mammy hadn't any money to get me anything,' explained Biddy.

Then ...

'BIDDY! BIDDY! B-I-D-D-Y!' somebody shouted.

'That's my Mammy!' said Biddy.

There was Biddy's Mammy coming up the path to the Castle, with a Great Big Birthday Cake with candles. And behind her was Kick-the-Ball with a parcel, and Baldy Hagen with a parcel, and Mrs Cook with a parcel, and Mrs Cafferty with three parcels, one from herself, and one from Wheezy Roberts, who couldn't get out of bed because of his broken leg, and another from Mrs McGlone, who had to stay behind in the Shop That Never Shuts, and couldn't get to Biddy's Birthday in the Birthday House.

'P-R-E-S-E-N-T-S!' said Biddy.

And she opened them all.

There were beads from Kick-the-Ball and sweeties from Baldy and hankies from Mrs Cook and a snow storm from Mrs Cafferty and a packet of crayons from Wheezy and a stick of rock from Mrs McGlone.

'All for me!' said Biddy.

'And there's one more, Biddy!' said Biddy's Mammy. 'A Big Surprise from me and all the neighbours!'

'It was McGlone's idea!' said Buster.

'Get it, McGlone!' said Biddy's Mammy.

And McGlone went off into the bushes, and came back with the Big Surprise.

It barked at Biddy!

It only made a wee tiny bark, because the big surprise was a wee tiny dog, but it had a collar on, and a little flappy tail that it flapped at Biddy.

'Mrs Cafferty's puppy,' said McGlone. 'The brown-and-white one you said you wanted!'

Biddy's Birthday

Biddy's Birthday

McGlone put Mrs Cafferty's puppy down in front of Biddy, and it wobbled round her, and licked Biddy's knee.

'Look at its wee eyes!' said McGlone.

'Look at its wee legs!' said Biddy.

'Just like yours,' said Biddy's Mammy. 'So it will always be along with you if the others forget and leave you behind.'

'It'll grow,' said Biddy. 'It will grow big legs.'

'So will you!' said Buster.

Then McGlone put a bit of string through the Big Surprise's collar, and Biddy and McGlone and Flash and Buster walked it.

'I'm going to call it Josephine!' Biddy said. Josephine stopped walking, and whimpered, and whimpered, and sat down and looked at Biddy.

'It's your wee legs are the trouble!' Biddy told Josephine, and she bent down and picked the puppy up and carried her all the way back to the bed Biddy's Mammy had made for her in an egg box in front of the fire in Biddy's house.

McGlone and Buster and Flash and Biddy sat and watched, until Josephine stopped chewing the egg box, and went to sleep.

'I wish we had a dog,' said Flash.

'Well, we haven't,' said Buster.

'You can all share mine!' said Biddy.

'You're a great girl, Biddy!' said McGlone.

'You know what?' said Biddy.

Biddy's Birthday

'What?' said McGlone.

'This is the Best Birthday Ever!' said Biddy.

And the McGlone Gang agreed that she'd got it right!